ROYAL REEDS

Tales of Intense Desire Vol. 2

Volume 2

Contents

I   The Neighbor

Chapter 1   3
Chapter 2   7
Chapter 3   12
Chapter 4   17
Chapter 5   20
Chapter 6   24

II   The Maid

Chapter 7   35
Chapter 8   41

III   The Obsession

Chapter 9   49
Chapter 10   54
Chapter 11   58
Chapter 12   64

Also by Royal Reeds   67

I

The Neighbor

Chapter 1

The box in my arms was heavier than I expected. Sweat trickled down my back as I adjusted my grip, trying to make it through this one last trip. The truck was almost empty now, and soon this place—my new apartment—would officially be mine. No more sleeping in my childhood bedroom. No more tiptoeing around nosy roommates. Just me, my stuff, and a fresh start.

My legs ached, my muscles burned, and I was pretty sure I'd already pulled something in my shoulder, but I refused to give in. With a grunt, I shuffled into the lobby, balancing the cardboard monstrosity in my hands. A sleek silver elevator waited at the end of the hall, its doors wide open like a lifeline. Thank God. I staggered inside, panting a little as I nudged the ground-floor button with my elbow.

The elevator hummed softly, and I leaned against the wall, trying to catch my breath.

"Almost there, girl," I whispered to myself. "Just a few more boxes, and you're home."

The ride was smooth—too smooth. Before I knew it, the elevator jerked slightly, announcing its arrival on my floor. I hoisted the box up again, trying to step forward gracefully, but luck was not on my side. My foot snagged on the edge of the door, and the world tilted beneath me.

"Shit!"

I stumbled forward, box slipping from my grip, heart lurching into my throat. Just as I braced for impact, a warm, firm hand shot out and caught my elbow.

"Whoa, easy there."

I gasped and looked up—straight into the most mesmerizing pair of green eyes I had ever seen. They were vibrant, sharp, with flecks of gold hidden in the irises. His dark hair, glossy and thick, fell slightly across his forehead in lazy curtains that gave him an effortless, devil-may-care charm. He smiled, a slow, easy grin that made my heart stutter in my chest.

"You okay?" he asked, his voice low and smooth, like he had all the time in the world.

It took me a second—maybe more than a second—to find my voice. "Uh, yeah. Yeah, I'm good. Thanks."

His hand lingered on my elbow for just a beat longer than necessary, and I found myself wishing it would stay. But then, as if realizing the same, he let go, and I felt the warmth of his touch disappear.

I bent to pick up the box, but he beat me to it, easily hoisting it into his arms as though it weighed nothing.

"Got it," he said, giving me a wink. "Moving day, huh?"

I nodded, still a bit flustered. "Yeah. New start and all that."

"Well, you're off to an interesting one." His grin widened, playful but not unkind. "Eric Turner."

I blinked, trying to pull myself together. "Oh. Uh, I'm… I'm Mia."

"Nice to meet you, Mia," Eric said, his voice curling around my name like a secret. He stepped back into the elevator, still holding the box. "You've got the rest of your stuff in here?"

I shook my head quickly. "No, this one's for my apartment just down the hall."

He gave me one last smile, an easy nod that said he was used to helping damsels in distress—or maybe just making them feel off balance. "Good luck with the unpacking."

Before I could say anything else—hell, before I could figure out how to make words work again—he stepped back into the elevator. The doors slid closed, and he was gone.

I stood there for a moment, blinking at the spot where he'd just been, my heart pounding in my chest.

Eric Turner. Green eyes, curtain hair, lean and tall, with the kind of face that could ruin a girl's plans for independence.

Well.

This is going to be interesting.

I carried the box the short distance to my door, fumbling with the key until it clicked open. The apartment was small but cozy, with just enough sunlight filtering through the windows to make it feel warm and inviting. I dropped the box onto the floor and let out a long breath, running a hand through my hair.

A new city. A new apartment. And already, a dangerously handsome neighbor who'd knocked the breath right out of me.

I stared at the closed door for a moment, wondering if I'd see him again anytime soon.

Please let him not be a ghost I just hallucinated.

With a shake of my head, I forced myself to focus. There were boxes to unpack, things to arrange, and a whole new life waiting to be built. I'd figure out Eric Turner later. Maybe.

Or maybe I'd just let the universe handle it.

Yeah. That sounded safer.

At least for now.

Chapter 2

It had been a few days since the elevator incident, and Eric Turner hadn't crossed my path since—at least not in person. But that didn't mean he was far from my thoughts. I kept replaying that moment: the way his fingers had steadied me, his easy smile, the rich, teasing cadence of his voice.

Now, I was sitting on my tiny balcony with a book in hand, trying to read, though I was mostly flipping pages without absorbing anything. The cool evening breeze helped with the heat, but the summer humidity still lingered. I sipped from my water bottle and stretched my legs out, letting the calm of the city at dusk wash over me.

It was peaceful, just the quiet hum of distant cars and the occasional sound of a bird fluttering by.

And then I heard it—a deep, rumbling growl of a motorcycle cutting through the evening stillness.

Curious, I lowered my book and leaned forward. A sleek black motorcycle pulled into the complex parking lot, and on it was none other than Eric Turner.

I watched, lips parting slightly as he killed the engine and swung his leg off the bike in one fluid motion. He pulled off his helmet, shaking his hair loose, the dark strands messy from the ride. My heart did a little flip as he wiped the sweat from his forehead with the back of his hand, revealing the toned lines of his arms beneath his snug black T-shirt.

He wore dark jeans that hugged his lean frame and boots that looked perfectly worn-in, the kind that said he'd lived a little. He looked effortlessly sexy, like he'd just stepped out of a dream—or the kind of trouble you weren't supposed to think about for too long.

And then his eyes lifted—straight to me.

Our gazes locked.

For a second, I was frozen, caught in those piercing green eyes again. Eric smiled, a slow, crooked grin that made it hard to remember how to breathe. He gave me a small wave, casual and easy, like it was perfectly normal to catch someone spying on you from their balcony.

I flushed, feeling a little ridiculous, but I waved back shyly, my hand moving without permission.

Eric gave me a brief nod, slung his helmet under one arm, and turned toward the entrance to the building. I watched him walk away, the low thud of his boots against the pavement fading as he disappeared into the complex.

I stayed on the balcony a moment longer, heart beating a little too fast for my liking. I should've looked away sooner, but it was hard to resist the pull of someone so effortlessly magnetic. He was the kind of guy who could throw your entire life off track if you let him.

I told myself I'd just go back to reading my book. And I tried. I really did. But the words blurred on the page, my mind still lingering on the man with green eyes and a devilish grin.

Later that night, I drove to grab some takeout. Thai food, because I was too exhausted to cook and I deserved comfort noodles after a long day of unpacking and pretending to be productive.

The elevator doors dinged softly as I returned to my floor, balancing a bag of takeout in one hand and fumbling with my keys in the other. I stepped out, thinking only about dinner and how fast I could get into my pajamas, when something caught my attention from the corner of my eye.

Across the hall, Eric was pressed up against his door—and he wasn't alone.

A woman, tall and curvy, had her arms wrapped around his neck, her fingers tangled in his hair. She wore a tiny black dress that left little to the imagination, and the way she was clinging to him made it obvious that things were heading in a very specific direction.

I stopped dead in my tracks, heat rushing to my face.

Eric's hands were on her hips, pulling her closer as she kissed him with the kind of passion that belonged in a movie—not in a hallway where anyone could walk by.

Including me.

Shit. I needed to move, but my feet wouldn't cooperate. The smart thing to do was to pretend I didn't see anything, get into my apartment, and forget this moment ever happened. But my body wasn't listening to my brain, and before I could help it, my eyes locked onto Eric again.

As if he could sense me, he broke the kiss and glanced in my direction. His gaze sharpened the second he saw me standing there, frozen with a bag of takeout in my hand.

"Mia," he said, his voice low, a little breathless.

My cheeks burned, and I stammered, "I—I didn't mean to interrupt."

The woman let out an annoyed scoff, clearly unimpressed by the sudden pause in their make-out session. She turned to look at me, her expression sharp with irritation.

"Who's she?" she asked, her voice thick with impatience.

Eric ignored her question, taking a step toward me, like he wanted to explain—or maybe apologize.

"Mia, wait a second—"

"No, it's fine," I said quickly, waving him off, feeling more embarrassed by the second. "Really. I didn't see anything."

I forced a smile, though it felt awkward on my face, and tried to focus on unlocking my door as fast as possible. My hands fumbled with the keys, and I could feel both of their eyes on me—hers filled with irritation, his with something I couldn't quite place.

Finally, the lock clicked, and I pushed the door open with more force than necessary.

"Have a good night," I mumbled, not daring to look back at either of them.

Before Eric could say anything else, I slipped inside and closed the door behind me, leaning against it with a sigh of relief.

My heart was racing, and not in a good way this time.

I stood there for a moment, clutching the bag of takeout, trying to shake off the strange tangle of emotions swirling in my chest. Disappointment? Embarrassment? Jealousy? I wasn't even sure why I cared. It wasn't like Eric owed me anything. We weren't friends. We were barely acquaintances.

And yet…

I squeezed my eyes shut and let out a long breath. "Get a grip, Mia," I whispered to myself.

From the other side of the door, I heard the sound of low voices—hers, still annoyed, and his, quiet but firm. A few moments later, the sound of a door clicking shut told me that they'd gone inside.

I exhaled slowly, shaking my head.

Whatever that was, it wasn't my business.

I set the takeout on the counter, grabbed a fork, and told myself I wasn't going to think about Eric Turner for the rest of the night.

Easier said than done.

Chapter 3

It had been a few days since I last saw Eric, and I was starting to wonder if the universe was doing me a favor. The memory of that hallway encounter was still fresh in my mind—and way too embarrassing to think about for long. Every time the scene replayed in my head, my cheeks flamed all over again. Not just because I'd walked in on him making out with some girl, but because I cared.

And I shouldn't care. At all.

So, I buried myself in work, picking up extra shifts and coming home too tired to think about anything other than collapsing into bed. It worked—mostly. At least until tonight.

After my shift ended, I dragged myself through the door, kicked off my shoes, and headed straight for a shower. The hot water was bliss, washing away the stress of the day and soothing my aching muscles. I stood under the spray longer than I should've, letting the steam cloud my thoughts, until my fingers pruned and I reluctantly turned off the water.

Wrapped in a towel, I padded into the living room and began flipping through the stack of mail I'd grabbed from the box earlier. A few bills, junk flyers, and a glossy coupon booklet I'd probably never use. I kept sifting through until my fingers stopped on an envelope with a different name.

Eric Turner.

I blinked down at the envelope. There were two more pieces addressed to him—one an official-looking letter, the other a postcard from somewhere tropical. I frowned, realizing the mail lady must've mixed up our boxes.

For a second, I debated just leaving the mail on my counter. He'd get it eventually, right? But then guilt pricked at me. It was probably important, and the last thing I needed was karma coming back to bite me for holding onto it.

I threw on a loose T-shirt and shorts, still warm from the shower, and grabbed the small stack of mail. My hair was damp, and I didn't bother with makeup— who cared? I wasn't planning on hanging around long. Just a quick delivery and back to my quiet, Eric-free bubble.

Steeling myself, I walked across the hall and knocked on his door.

At first, there was no response. I shifted on my feet, suddenly feeling ridiculous standing there with a handful of his mail. I knocked again, quieter this time.

After a few moments, the door swung open—and there he was.

Eric stood in the doorway, panting slightly, his chest rising and falling as if he'd just run a marathon. Sweat clung to his skin, making his black T-shirt stick to the lean lines of his torso. His hair was damp, messy from either exertion or frustration, and he ran a hand through it, pushing it back from his face.

I blinked, my brain short-circuiting at the sight of him.

He looked…

Well, he looked exactly like someone who'd been very busy—and not with something innocent.

"Hey," he said, his voice a little breathless, like he was trying to catch his composure. His green eyes settled on mine, and a lazy grin curved his lips, as if he knew exactly how flustered I was. "What's up?"

I could feel heat creeping up my neck, and I knew my face was probably the color of a tomato. I held up the stack of envelopes like a shield. "Uh—your mail. I think the mail lady messed up. These were in my box."

His gaze flicked to the letters, and for a second, I swore I saw amusement flash in his eyes. He leaned casually against the doorframe, still catching his breath, and took the mail from my hands.

"Thanks," he said, his voice low, rough in a way that made my stomach do a weird little flip.

I tried to respond—maybe something like "No problem"—but the words stuck in my throat. All I could think about was how close we were, the smell of his skin—clean, with a hint of sweat—and how the memory of him pressed against his door with another woman flashed uninvited in my mind.

I needed to leave. Now.

"I, uh, didn't mean to interrupt," I blurted, feeling like the biggest idiot on the planet.

Eric's grin deepened, the corner of his mouth quirking in a way that made me wish the ground would swallow me whole. "You didn't," he said smoothly, though the glint in his eyes told me otherwise.

His tone was easy, but it didn't help my embarrassment. If anything, it made it worse.

"Well, okay. Um. I'll just—" I gestured vaguely toward my door, practically tripping over my own feet as I tried to back away.

"Mia," Eric said, amusement lacing his voice.

I froze for a second, daring a glance up at him.

He was watching me with that same easy grin, but there was something else in his expression now—something curious, like he wasn't quite ready to let me disappear.

"Thanks for bringing these over," he added, giving the stack of mail a little shake.

I nodded too quickly, my face burning. "Sure. No problem."

Before he could say anything else—or worse, ask me anything—I turned on my heel and practically fled back to my apartment.

I fumbled with my keys, heart racing, and threw the door open. Once I was safely inside, I leaned against it, exhaling in one big, mortified breath.

What the hell was that?

I stood there for a moment, trying to calm the frantic beat of my heart. The memory of Eric's panting breath, the way his shirt clung to his skin, and that damn smirk were all etched into my mind—and they weren't going anywhere anytime soon.

I squeezed my eyes shut and let out a groan.

This was becoming a problem.

Chapter 4

The sun had long since set, casting my new apartment in shadows. I tossed and turned in bed, unable to shake the image from my mind. Earlier that evening, I'd seen Eric in the hallway, his arms wrapped around a statuesque blonde. Their lips had been locked in a passionate kiss, oblivious to the world around them. My stomach had churned, a mixture of jealousy and disappointment flooding through me.

Now, alone in the darkness, I couldn't stop thinking about it. About him. His strong hands, those captivating green eyes, the way his smile made my heart race. I imagined those hands on me, those lips exploring my skin. A familiar warmth spread through my body, settling low in my belly.

With a frustrated groan, I reached for my nightstand drawer. My fingers closed around the smooth silicone of my vibrator, and I hesitated for just a moment before pulling it out. I hadn't used it since moving in, but tonight… tonight I needed the release.

I closed my eyes, letting my imagination take over. In my mind, it wasn't the vibrator touching me, but Eric's fingers. They trailed along my inner thighs, teasing, exploring. I gasped as I switched it on, the low hum filling the quiet room. Slowly, I traced it over my most sensitive areas, shivers of pleasure racing through me.

My back arched as I imagined Eric's mouth replacing the vibrator, his tongue swirling and flicking my clit.

The vibrations were becoming more intense, and I could feel the familiar heat building deep within me. My breath hitched as my mind conjured up the image of Eric's head between my legs, his dark hair tickling my thighs.

His tongue flicked against my sensitive skin, and I moaned loudly, arching into his touch. His fingers found their way inside of me, filling me slowly while his lips suckled on my clit like it was a delicious treat. I bucked wildly against his mouth, feeling the walls of my pussy squeezing around his fingers. The combination of his warmth and the vibrations sent shockwaves of pleasure throughout my body.

With each passing moment, I felt myself becoming more lost in the fantasy. The rhythm of our bodies synced perfectly; our breaths mingled together in the air. My hips rocked back and forth, seeking out more of his touch, more of the exquisite sensations coursing through me.

His tongue circling faster around my clit. It was too much, but somehow not enough. Never enough. I bit my lower lip hard, trying to stifle my cries as the pleasure threatened to consume me.

The heady scent of sweat and desire filled the air, mingling with the musky smell of sex that hung heavy between us. Our hearts pounded in unison as he pushed another finger inside me, stretching me further than I thought possible. I cried out again, this time unable to contain myself. My orgasm hit me like a wave crashing.

I snapped my eyes open, heart pounding. What was I doing? Fantasizing about a man I barely knew, a man who was clearly involved with someone else? This wasn't me. This wasn't why I'd moved here, started this new chapter of my life.

With a frustrated sigh, I switched off the vibrator and tossed it aside.

Embarrassed and frustrated, I rolled onto my side, pulling the covers up to my chin. The room felt too warm, too stuffy, and I kicked off the blankets, letting the cool air wash over my flushed skin. My heart was still racing, my body tingling with unfulfilled desire.

I closed my eyes, willing sleep to come, but my mind wouldn't quiet. Images of Eric kept flashing through my thoughts—his easy smile, those captivating green eyes, the way his shirt had clung to his broad shoulders. I groaned, burying my face in the pillow.

This was ridiculous. I was here to start fresh, to focus on my career and myself. Not to pine after some guy I'd barely met, especially one who was clearly taken. I needed to get it together.

Determined to clear my head, I focused on my breathing, trying to slow my racing thoughts. I imagined myself on a quiet beach, waves lapping gently at the shore. The sound of the ocean filled my ears, drowning out the memory of Eric's low, smooth voice. Slowly, gradually, I felt myself starting to relax.

As sleep finally began to claim me, my last coherent thought was a silent prayer that I wouldn't run into Eric again anytime soon.

The universe, it seemed, had other plans.

Chapter 5

The rain poured in sheets, drumming against the pavement and turning the city into a hazy, glimmering blur. By the time I pulled into the parking lot and stepped out of my car, I was soaked through. My thin jacket did little to stop the downpour, and the chill clung to my skin as I hurried toward the entrance of the building.

Just as I reached the door, it swung open, and there he was—Eric Turner.

He stepped inside from the rain at the exact same moment as I did, his black boots thudding softly on the mat. His dark hair was wet, sticking to his forehead, and a few drops of water trailed down his sharp jawline. He glanced over at me, and for a second, neither of us said a word.

"Hey," I muttered, pushing a damp strand of hair out of my face.

"Hey." His voice was low, and I felt it like a slow ripple down my spine.

I stepped into the elevator, and to my mild horror, Eric followed. The doors slid shut behind us with a soft hiss, trapping us in the small space together.

The hum of the elevator was the only sound between us as we stood side by side, both dripping wet. The tension was thick—awkward, charged, and impossible to ignore. I tried to focus on the numbers lighting up above the door, counting the floors as we ascended, but I could feel his presence beside me, warm despite the rain.

I shifted slightly, hugging my arms around myself in an attempt to seem casual. "Crazy weather, huh?" I offered lamely.

Eric gave a low chuckle, and it was a sound that sent a strange, restless heat through me. "Yeah. You looked like you were ready to swim out there."

I laughed, though it was more nervous than genuine. "Feels like it."

The elevator doors slid open at our floor, and I moved to step out, my heart thumping faster than it should've. But as I reached my door, Eric's voice stopped me.

"Mia."

I froze, turning slowly to face him. He stood in front of his apartment door, one hand casually gripping the doorknob, the other tucked into the pocket of his jeans. His eyes gleamed, dark with something I couldn't quite place—something dangerous.

"Do you want to come over?" he asked, his voice smooth and soft, like an invitation to trouble.

My pulse jumped at the question, and for a second, I just stared at him, caught off guard. I opened my mouth to answer, but no words came out.

Did I want to?
  Yes.
  Should I?
  Probably not.

"No," I whispered, but my voice wavered, betraying me.

The corner of Eric's mouth curled into a smirk, like he knew exactly what I was thinking. He took a step closer, the space between us narrowing until I could feel the warmth of him despite the rain clinging to both of us.

He leaned in, close enough that I could feel his breath ghost across my skin. His hand braced against the wall beside my head, caging me in without touching me.

"Come over," he murmured, the words not a question but an order, soft and deliberate. "Thirty minutes."

My heart stuttered in my chest.

I nodded—barely, just the smallest tilt of my head.

Eric's smirk deepened, satisfied, and he pushed off the wall, leaving me breathless in his wake. "See you soon, Mia," he said, his voice low and teasing as he unlocked his door.

I didn't wait to see him go inside. I turned, scrambled with my keys, and shoved my door open like the apartment was a lifeboat and I was drowning.

Once inside, I leaned against the door, my heart pounding so loud I could hear it in my ears.

What the hell was I doing?

Without giving myself a chance to think about it, I kicked off my wet shoes and hurried to the bathroom, stripping out of my soaked clothes on the way. I stood under the shower, letting the hot water wash away the chill of the rain—and maybe, just maybe, the growing ache that had settled in my chest since the moment I looked into Eric Turner's eyes.

Thirty minutes. That was all I had to pull myself together.

And God help me—I knew I wasn't going to make it out of this night unscathed.

Chapter 6

I sat on my couch, legs tucked under me, the soft glow of my phone lighting up the dark room. The clock ticked closer to thirty minutes, each second stretching longer than the last. My heart pounded in anticipation, nerves buzzing in my veins like static electricity. I stared at the numbers on the screen as if they would tell me what to do, as if they could somehow stop the wild thoughts racing through my mind.

When the time finally hit 30 minutes exactly, I stood up before I could change my mind.

I slipped out of my apartment, closing the door softly behind me. The hallway was dim and quiet, except for the faint hum of rain drumming against the windows. His door was just a few steps away, and my heart felt like it was trying to punch through my ribs with every step I took.

When I reached Eric's door, I knocked—just once.

The door swung open almost immediately, and there he was, as if he'd been waiting on the other side the whole time.

Eric stood barefoot, wearing nothing but a pair of dark pajama bottoms slung low on his hips. His hair was damp, the edges curling slightly from the moisture, and a few drops of water clung to his skin, glinting under the hallway light. He looked like sin made flesh, and the lazy smile on his lips only made him more dangerous.

"Right on time," he said, his voice low and warm, like a slow-burning flame.

I swallowed hard, nerves bubbling in my chest. He stepped aside, holding the door open wider.

"Come in."

I hesitated for half a second—but only half. Then I stepped inside, and the door clicked shut behind me, locking out the rest of the world.

His apartment was dimly lit, the soft glow of a lamp casting warm shadows across the room. A bottle of wine and two glasses sat on the small coffee table, already opened and waiting. Eric poured a glass for each of us and handed me one, his fingers brushing mine for a brief, electric moment.

"To new neighbors," he said with a grin, lifting his glass in a toast.

I clinked mine against his, feeling the weight of his gaze on me as I took a sip. The wine was rich and smooth, but I barely tasted it. All I could focus on was the sound of his voice—low, husky, and entirely too seductive as he talked about nothing and everything.

He asked me about work, about how I liked the apartment so far, and every word felt like a secret shared between just the two of us. The way he spoke, slow and deliberate, made it impossible to look away.

At some point, we ended up on the couch, side by side, the air thick with tension. I knew where this was going—I knew from the moment I knocked on his door. And yet, knowing didn't stop the ache building inside me, didn't stop the way my skin burned under his gaze.

Eric shifted closer, his knee brushing against mine. I felt his warmth, his presence wrapping around me like a net I didn't want to escape. His hand rested lightly on my thigh, and I held my breath as his fingers began to trace slow, lazy circles along my skin.

The touch was maddeningly soft, just the barest brush of his fingertips, but it lit me up like a spark to dry kindling.

"You're tense," he murmured, his voice a low rasp that made my stomach flutter.

I let out a shaky laugh, trying—and failing—to ignore the way my pulse raced. "Wonder why."

Eric smiled, the kind of smile that said he knew exactly what he was doing to me. His fingers continued their slow path, tracing higher, his touch light and teasing, as if he had all the time in the world.

"Relax," he whispered, leaning in closer until his breath grazed my ear. "You're not going anywhere."

I didn't know if it was a promise or a warning, but it didn't matter. The rest of the world fell away, and all that existed was the heat between us.

His hand slid higher, and I couldn't hold back the soft gasp that escaped my lips. Eric's grin deepened at the sound, a wicked gleam in his eyes.

The wineglass slipped from my hand and landed on the coffee table with a soft clink, forgotten in an instant. Before I could think—before I could stop myself—my hands found his shoulders, fingers curling into the warm, solid muscle beneath his skin.

Eric didn't hesitate. His lips crashed into mine, hot and demanding, and all the tension that had been simmering between us exploded in an instant.

His kiss was passionate and intense, his tongue teasing my lips before pressing past to explore my mouth fully. My heart hammered against my chest as I responded to his advances, opening up to him. His hand moved up my spine, causing goosebumps to rise on my skin, and he gripped my hair lightly, pulling me closer.

I ran my fingers through his damp hair, loving the silky texture beneath my fingertips. The rain continued to drum outside, adding to the sensual atmosphere.

Our tongues tangled together as we tasted each other deeper, our bodies melting into one another's. His strong arms wrapped around me tightly, trapping me against his heated form. His other hand glided up my thigh, taking its time as it explored the soft skin beneath my dress.

I arched into his touch, letting out a moan that seemed to echo off the walls. The fabric of our clothes rustled with every movement, amplifying the sound of our breathing.

He pulled back slightly to look at me, eyes dark and hungry. "You're so beautiful," he murmured before leaning in for another kiss that left me breathless. His hand slid higher on my thigh, pushing the fabric upwards slowly until it disappeared from view.

Then he grasped the band of my panties and slid them to the side, exposing me completely to his touch. My cheeks flushed with heat at his boldness but also with excitement as he started exploring me so intimately for the first time.

I felt a shiver run through me as Eric's fingers danced along my sensitive skin; I couldn't help but press myself against him in response. The scent of his cologne filled my nostrils - sharp yet woodsy with hints of musk.

"Lay down," he whispered as he guided me down onto the couch.

As I laid down on the couch, my heart pounding in my chest, I watched as Eric climbed on top of me, his thick member already pushing against the fabric of his pajama bottoms. He stared down at me with eyes that were both predatory and tender, filled with a desire that mirrored my own. His hand slid up my inner thigh, pushing the fabric aside to expose me fully to him.

The touch sent shivers down my spine as he traced slow circles around my entrance before finally slipping one finger inside me.

I gasped at the sensation, arching into his touch as he fingerfucked me slowly and deliberately. His other hand found one of my breasts, massaging it gently through the fabric of my dress before pulling it down to expose my nipple to the cool air in the room. He took it between his lips and began to suckle hard as he continued to probe deeper inside me with his finger.

"Yesss," I whispered.

The sensations were overwhelming—the feeling of being owned and desired in this moment was almost too much to bear. Eric's tongue flicked over my nipple while his finger twisted and turned inside me, seeking out my sweet spot. My hips bucked against him instinctively, begging for more contact.

"You like that?" he asked with a smirk, looking up at me.

I nodded frantically, unable to speak through the haze of passion that had taken over me. Eric chuckled softly before removing his finger from me reluctantly.

"Spread your legs for me, as far as you can go, Mia,"

I nodded, slipping my underwear off entirely and spreading my legs for him. He groaned and palmed his hard cock. Then he lowered his head between my legs. His lips surrounded my throbbing clit and he suckled. I cried out, arching my back off the couch.

My body trembled as he licked, sucked, and teased my tender folds.

I gasped as took my clit into his mouth once more, his hot tongue flicking over it in a rhythm that sent shivers down my spine. The sensation was overwhelmingly intense, my entire body shook with each flick of his tongue.

Fuck he was good at this.

I dug my fingers into the couch cushions beneath me, trying to ground myself in the moment.

"Fuck," Eric groaned against my pulsing clit, drawing out the word as if he were tasting it with every syllable. His free hand found its way to my other breast, squeezing it gently through my dress.

Eric's expert touch was mind-blowing, his tongue dancing against my sensitive folds like a skilled lover. As he worked his magic down below, I felt my body tensing up, readying for the inevitable release. The tension built slowly but surely, each groan and moan escaping my lips adding fuel to the fire.

My hips bucked off the couch, seeking more of his expert touch. He wrapped a hand around my thigh, holding me down gently but firmly as he continued to pleasure me.

His tongue pressed against my swollen clit one last time before pulling away, eliciting a high-pitched whimper from me. He looked up at me with hooded eyes, a wicked grin forming on his lips. He pulled down the waistband of his bottoms and his cock sprang free.

My eyes widen at the sight of him. He was beautiful, long, and veiny.

In one swift motion, he positioned his hard cock at my entrance and pushed inside me.

The sensation of being filled by him was overwhelming but in the best possible way. Every nerve ending lit up at his intrusion as he started moving in and out of me slowly, the friction sending waves of pleasure coursing through my veins. His hand found mine, interlocking our fingers as he picked up the pace.

"I love it," I whimpered as he thrust into me.

He grinned, his eyes shining with triumph. "You like that, Mia?" His voice was rough with desire, and his hips picked up the pace, driving deeper into me with each thrust. The couch creaked with each thrust in rhythm with their movements.

I bit my lip to muffle my moans, my body arching off the couch in response to his powerful strokes. The sensation was unlike anything I'd ever felt before - raw and intense and overwhelmingly pleasurable. My fingers dug into his skin as he pushed me higher and higher towards the edge.

"More," I gasped out between pants.

He leaned down to capture one of my nipples in his mouth, sucking hard while he continued to pound into me.

Eric moved faster now, pulling almost all the way out of me before pushing back in with a groan that vibrated through me. The friction was exquisite torture; every stroke dragging a deep moan from my throat. My nails raked down his back leaving red marks.

"I'm coming Eric!"

My body tensed up as the first wave of pleasure washed over me. Eric's powerful strokes didn't stop, he kept going until I could barely breathe. My toes curled, my fingers dug into his shoulders. My walls clenched around him, milking his cock as I orgasmed in his arms.

He groaned against my skin, the vibrations sending shivers down my spine. His hips bucked wildly, pushing deeper inside me as he found his own release. Quickly he pulled out of me, and spilled his seed on my inner thigh.

We stared at each other for a moment, panting heavily in the aftermath of our passion. The air reeked of sex and alcohol, and I couldn't help but feel embarrassed about how loud we must have been.

But Eric didn't seem to mind; he just pulled me onto his chest, wrapping an arm around me tightly. We lay there in silence for what felt like hours, our hearts still racing from the intensity of it all. The rain continued to drum against the window panes outside but it went unnoticed between us now.

Eventually, I pushed myself away from him gently; we both knew this wasn't supposed to happen between neighbors—but right now all that mattered was the way our bodies had just come together in perfect harmony.

Eric watched me with hooded eyes as I got up and slowly dressed myself back up again. He stayed where he was, not making any move to cover himself or hide his arousal from view. It was both exhilarating and terrifying at the same time.

"Fuck that was amazing," he chuckled.

I smiled shyly, still feeling the afterglow of our encounter. "It really was."

Eric sat up, running a hand through his tousled hair. "So... same time tomorrow night?"

My breath caught in my throat. The responsible part of me knew I should say no, that this was dangerous territory with a neighbor. But the way he looked at me, with that devilish grin and those hungry eyes, made it impossible to refuse.

"Same time tomorrow," I agreed, my voice barely above a whisper.

He stood up, still gloriously naked, and walked me to the door. Before I could leave, he pulled me in for one last searing kiss that left me weak in the knees.

"Sweet dreams, Mia," he murmured against my lips.

I slipped out into the hallway, my legs still shaky. As I made my way back to my apartment, I could feel Eric's eyes on me. I glanced back just before entering my door, catching his gaze. The look he gave me was full of promise for what was to come.

Once inside, I leaned against my closed door, heart racing. What had I gotten myself into? And more importantly, how long could I keep this up before it consumed me entirely?

As I crawled into bed that night, I knew sleep would be elusive. My body still hummed from Eric's touch, and my mind raced with thoughts of what tomorrow night would bring. One thing was certain - my life in this apartment building would never be the same.

II

The Maid

Chapter 7

K *nock Knock*

"Come in," I called to the other person on the other side of the door. The door opened and my butler, George walked in with a stack of mail in his gloved hands. "Sir, I have today's mail,"

I nodded and pointed to the corner of my large mahogany desk. "Leave it there,"

He nodded and placed the stack on the desk and began to walk to the door. Then he stopped and turned back to me.

"Have you seen Jessica, Mr. Pearson?"

"Not since lunch," I responded without looking up from my computer. George didn't say anything else and then left.

I leaned my head back on my office chair and let out a moan I had been holding back.

"You didn't make a sound, good girl," I chuckled as I looked down between his legs.

Jessica sat between my legs, her full lips wrapped around my cock.

Jessica's warmth engulfed my manhood, her velvety tongue tracing every ridge and vein of my shaft. She looked up at me, her cheeks hollowed out as she took me deeper into her mouth, her brown eyes meeting mine. A small string of saliva connected us as she worshipped my member with devoted zeal.

I closed my eyes, savoring the sensation of her lips sliding up and down on my shaft, feeling the soft caress of her hands on my thighs. The sound of gagging filled the room every time she reached the back of her throat, and she would look up at me again with a mix of pleasure and submission. Her black hair swayed slightly as she bobbed her head up and down in rhythm with each bounce of my chair.

The scent of expensive cologne mixed with the faint aroma of her perfume filled the air, creating an intoxicating blend that heightened my arousal. It was intoxicating to watch Jessica serve me like this; she had been doing so for months now, ever since I rescued her from a life of poverty on the streets.

She knew what was expected of her when I called for her, and she never disappointed me. Every inch of my cock disappeared into her throat before she pulled back just enough to allow some air to fill her lungs before taking me deeper once again.

Her eager eyes never left mine as she suckled me, signaling that she wanted more, needed more. Slowly, I removed my hands from behind my head and placed them on her hair instead, guiding her movements as I started thrusting into her willing mouth.

Jessica moaned softly around my cock, the vibrations sending shivers of pleasure up my spine. I tightened my grip on her hair, controlling her pace as I thrust deeper into her throat. She relaxed her jaw, allowing me to use her mouth as I pleased.

The risk of being caught only heightened the thrill. I glanced at the door, half-expecting George to walk in at any moment. The thought made my cock twitch in Jessica's mouth.

"That's it," I growled softly. "Take it all."

Her eyes watered as she struggled to accommodate my full length, but she didn't pull away. Her dedication to pleasing me was unwavering. I felt the familiar tightening in my balls, signaling my approaching climax.

"I'm close," I warned her, my voice husky with desire.

Jessica redoubled her efforts, her tongue swirling around my shaft as she bobbed her head faster. I bit back a groan, not wanting to alert anyone outside the office. My hips bucked involuntarily as I neared the edge.

With a final, deep thrust, I exploded into her waiting mouth. Jessica swallowed eagerly, not spilling a drop as she milked me dry. I panted heavily, coming down from my high as she gently licked me clean.

"Good girl," I murmured, stroking her hair affectionately.

She crawled from under the desk and stood beside me. I waited, she knew what I wanted and my cock began to rise again in anticipation. Jessica lifted her uniform and exposed her bare pussy to me, slick slid down her thighs and I licked my lips. She knew how to please me. No panties, just how I like her.

"Good girl," I praised again, as I stroked my throbbing cock.

She blushed and climbed on top of my lap, she grinded her pussy along my length. I bit my lip and grabbed her waist.

"Make me come before someone comes in and sees you fucking your boss," I tease.

As Jessica positioned herself on top of me, her warmth enveloped my throbbing cock. She slowly sank down on my thighs, taking me inside her pussy with a moan of pleasure. Her soft, supple walls gripped me tightly, and she began to ride me slowly at first, grinding against my hips in a sensual rhythm. Her breasts swayed temptingly as she moved.

I leaned back in my chair, enjoying the view of Jessica's body was undulating on top of mine. Her black hair cascaded down her back like a waterfall as she moved in sync with my hips. Every time she reached the bottom of her stroke, she looked up at me with pleading eyes, begging for more. I could feel her wetness coating my thighs as she rode me harder and faster. Her breasts bounced enticingly with each movement, and I reached out to cup one of them, feeling the firm weight in my hand.

I pulled on her nipple playfully through her uniform, and she let out a sharp gasp before biting her lip to stifle any further noise. Her pace increased as she felt me grow harder inside her.

"Sir, it feels so good," she whispered. "I'm close,"

"Cum for me, good girl," I growled, and she moaned in response. Her body rocked against mine, faster and harder, as she neared her climax.

Her breathing became ragged, her eyes closed tightly. And then, with a soft sigh of pleasure, Jessica's body convulsed around mine. Her pussy milked my cock in waves of ecstasy as she came undone with a loud moan that echoed through the room.

I watched her wriggle and squirm on top of me, feeling the heat from her skin against mine. Her mouth dropped open slightly in a silent scream of pleasure that made my heart race. Her walls squeezed tighter around my cock, pulling it in and out forcefully before releasing it with a pop that sent another wave of pleasure through both of us. Her muscles trembled beneath me as she rode out the wave of her orgasm.

Finally, she collapsed on top of me, panting heavily. Her chest heaved up and down rapidly as she caught her breath. I kissed her neck softly, nibbling on her earlobe before whispering in her ear: "You're so fucking beautiful when you come for me."

Her body shuddered again at my words; they sent another surge of desire through both of us. I couldn't hold back any longer; my own orgasm hit me like a freight train - hard and fast. I exploded inside her warmth with a hoarse cry that was muffled by her skin against my lips. My hips bucked upward involuntarily.

As we both came down from our shared climax, the sound of footsteps approaching the office door suddenly caught our attention. Jessica's eyes widened in panic as she quickly dismounted me and smoothed down her uniform. I hastily tucked myself back into my pants and straightened my tie, trying to regain my composure.

Just as Jessica ducked behind a nearby bookshelf, there was a knock at the door.

"Come in," I called out, my voice slightly strained.

George entered, his face impassive as always. "Mr. Pearson, your 3 o'clock appointment has arrived. Shall I show them in?"

I cleared my throat, acutely aware of Jessica's presence hidden just a few feet away. "Yes, thank you, George. Give me two minutes and then send them in."

As George nodded and turned to leave, his gaze lingered for a moment on the slightly askew papers on my desk. I held my breath, praying he wouldn't notice anything amiss.

"Very good, sir," he said finally, closing the door behind him.

I let out a sigh of relief and glanced over at Jessica, who was peeking out from behind the bookshelf with a mixture of excitement and nervousness on her flushed face.

"That was close," she whispered, a mischievous glint in her eye.

I couldn't help but smirk. "Indeed it was. Now, straighten yourself up and get out of here,"

Chapter 8

One night, I was sleeping soundly until I heard the light creaking sound of a door opening. I knew instantly who it was. Jessica. My maid.

Unfortunately for her, I'm a light sleeper and the slightest noise wakes me from sleep. I wanted to get up and ask her what she was doing here but I wanted to see what she was doing first. So I continued to lay motionless.

I could feel the bed dip as she crawled onto it from the foot of the bed. She made her way up and gently grabbed my blanket, slowly pulling it down.

Ah, so that's what she's up to.

I almost smirked but I managed to suppress it. She palmed my cock through my pj bottoms.

Jessica's warm breath hit my cock through my pajamas, causing me to shiver slightly even in my half-asleep state. The sensation was both surprising and arousing as she began to stroke it softly under the fabric. Her hand felt gentle and soothing on my skin, sending tingles of desire down my spine. Her long dark hair swayed gently around her face as she leaned in closer to tease me further. Her breasts pressed against my legs, the soft cotton fabric of her nightgown doing nothing to hide their fullness.

Her fingers slowly pushed the fabric down, revealing more of my hardened shaft until it sprung free from its confinement. She took it fully into her mouth, engulfing it with a soft moan that echoed in the nearly silent room.

Her tongue danced along the sensitive underside of my cock while her hand gripped it firmly at the base, stroking in perfect rhythm with her mouth. The feeling of her wet heat enveloping me was overwhelmingly pleasant; every thrust of her tongue sent waves of pleasure coursing through my body.

I could feel the bed dipping more heavily now as she took all of me into her mouth, sucking forcefully yet tenderly at the same time.

Her cheeks hollowed out each time she reached the back of her throat and I couldn't help but groan softly at this unexpected but highly welcome service from my maid.

It took all of me to not thrust my hips up and force my cock down her throat. God knows I wanted to but I wanted to see how far she would go.

And oh, fuck. This feels so good. So damn good. As she takes more of me into her mouth, I feel my heart race and my breathing become quicker. Her tongue swirls around the head of my cock, and I can't help but let out a moan. The sight of her long black hair swaying gently between us is hypnotic, adding to the dreamlike quality of the moment.

Her hand moves up to caress my balls lightly through the fabric of my pajamas, sending shivers down my spine. She cups it gently before sliding her hand back up to rub against the sensitive skin beneath my balls.

It feels like an erotic dance as she works her magic on me, all while her mouth goes up and down my throbbing length in perfect rhythm.

"Fuck," I moaned. I couldn't just lay here anymore. I needed to be inside her.

I reached down and fisted her hair, pulling her off my cock with a wet pop. "You are such a bad girl, Jessica,"

She moaned and sat up as I tugged on her hair.

"Please," She begged. I smirked and met her lustful gaze.

"And what is it you want?"

"Please, fuck me," she begged. In an instant, I released her hair, grabbed her by her shoulders, and forced her face down into my pillows.

Before she could realize what was happening I pushed her nightgown over her waist. I wasn't surprised to find her without underwear and already sopping wet. I lined up my cock at her entrance and slid deep inside her.

I bit my lip in pleasure as I felt her tight warmth engulf me, her wetness coating my tip. I thrust into her, feeling the velvety walls of her pussy squeeze and ripple around my shaft. She moaned loudly into the pillow as I began to pound into her, our hips slapping together in a rhythmic crescendo of lust.

Her mouth opened wider on a yelp as I slammed into her harder, hitting that spot deep inside that made her writhe and clench around me. I could feel her walls start to quiver with each powerful stroke, anticipating release.

"Yes," she whispered hoarsely between gasps for air, "Fuck me like that…oh god…I can't take much more."

Her words fueled my desire even further, and I picked up the pace even more until finally, we both came together in a symphony of moans and cries. Her pussy clamped down on my cock as she climaxed hard.

I moaned at the feeling of her milking my cock. I spilled my seed deep inside her. I didn't give a fuck if she got pregnant she was mine anyway.

I collapsed on top of her, both of us panting heavily as we came down from our intense orgasms. After a few moments, I rolled off to the side, pulling Jessica into my arms. She nuzzled against my chest, her breath warm on my skin.

We lay there in comfortable silence for a while, our bodies intertwined. The first light of dawn was starting to peek through the curtains when Jessica stirred.

"I should go," she whispered reluctantly. "The other staff will be arriving soon."

"Stay," I commanded softly, tightening my arm around her. "I don't care what the others think."

Jessica hesitated, her body tense against mine. I could sense her internal struggle - her desire to remain in my embrace warring with her sense of duty and propriety.

"But sir," she protested weakly, "what if someone sees? My position here..."

I silenced her with a deep, passionate kiss. When we finally broke apart, both breathless, I gazed into her eyes.

"Your position is right here, in my bed," I said firmly. "I've wanted you for so long, Jessica. Now that I have you, I'm not letting you go."

A small smile played at the corners of her mouth. "Really?" she asked, a hint of hope in her voice.

I nodded, running my fingers through her silky hair. "Really. In fact, I think it's time for a promotion. How does 'mistress of the house' sound?"

Jessica's eyes widened in shock, then softened with emotion. "Oh sir," she breathed, "I… I don't know what to say."

"Say yes," I murmured, pulling her closer. "Say you'll be mine, completely and utterly."

Instead of answering with words, Jessica pressed her lips to mine in a searing kiss. As our passion reignited, I knew that neither of us would be leaving this bed anytime soon.

III

The Obsession

Chapter 9

I adjusted the raincoat hood over my head, shielding myself as best I could from the downpour as I taped yet another "Missing Cat" poster to a telephone pole. Muffin had been missing for two days, and the pit in my stomach had only deepened with every empty street I combed and every corner I called her name.

The thought of her, alone and scared in this weather, made my heart ache. I'd been relentless, posting about her online, sharing her photo on every social media platform I could think of, hoping someone might have seen her. Each morning, I woke up dreading that she still hadn't come home. And each night, I went to bed feeling helpless, cursing myself for leaving that window open.

As I trudged back to my car, rain soaking through my jeans, my phone buzzed. I was almost afraid to hope.

Hey, I saw your post about Muffin. I think I found her. She's hurt but safe. I've been keeping an eye on her.

I blinked at the message, hardly daring to believe it. Her name was right there—Muffin—and after days of getting nothing but silence from anyone, here was someone claiming they'd actually found her. I quickly pulled up the profile picture of the man who sent the message. *Hunter Fraser.*

Curious, I clicked through his profile. Everything about it screamed wealth—

an elegant black-and-white profile photo, designer suits, images of sports cars, and sprawling landscapes that looked like they belonged in a movie. A few more swipes, and I realized he was one of those Frasers. I'd heard the name before, some big family that owned land and businesses all over the state. But I wasn't interested in his status—I just wanted my Muffin back.

I took a deep breath, typing a quick reply.

Oh my God, thank you so much! Where is she? Can I come pick her up?

He responded almost immediately.

I live outside of town, near the lake. She's here with me now, but it's pretty far from you, and the storm's only getting worse. Are you okay to drive in this weather?

I hesitated, watching as rain streaked down my windshield in torrents. But the thought of Muffin, hurt and waiting, won out over any second thoughts.

Yes. Just send me the address. I'll head over now.

My phone chimed with his reply a moment later.

I'll wait up for you. Be careful.

The message left me feeling strangely uneasy, but I pushed the thought aside. Muffin was close. All I had to do was drive through a bit of rain, and she'd be back in my arms, safe.

The drive was brutal. Rain lashed at my windows, thunder boomed, and lightning cracked the sky in flashes that made it hard to see. My GPS guided me to the outskirts of town, winding through narrow roads and thick woods that seemed to close in the further I went.

After what felt like an eternity, I finally spotted the estate, set back from the road and nearly hidden by tall iron gates and trees that swayed ominously in the storm. The gate was already open, and I drove through slowly, the crunch of gravel barely audible over the storm as I made my way up to the large, dark house.

The house was all sharp angles and sleek lines, the kind of modern design you'd see in architectural magazines. I parked near the front steps, heart pounding as I shut off the car. I was close, so close.

The front door opened, and there he was—Hunter Fraser himself, framed in the doorway, tall and imposing, with dark hair damp from the rain and eyes that seemed to watch me intently even from a distance. He had the look of someone who was both at ease and in control of everything around him.

"Gina, right?" His voice was deep and calm, cutting through the rain as I climbed out of the car.

"Yes! Thank you so much for contacting me. I can't tell you what this means to me," I said, nearly breathless with anticipation.

"Of course." He stepped aside, gesturing for me to come in. "Come on inside. She's in the guest room—I figured she needed some space to rest."

I stepped inside, dripping water on his pristine marble floors, but he didn't seem to mind. Instead, he walked with a confident ease through his cavernous home, leading me down a dim hallway lined with thick carpets and polished wooden walls.

Finally, he stopped outside a room, his hand on the doorknob. His eyes met mine, steady and unreadable. "She's doing okay, considering. I cleaned up her paw; it was scraped up pretty badly. She's resting now, but go ahead, see for yourself."

My heart swelled with gratitude. "Thank you, Hunter. Really."

He gave a slight nod, his lips curving into a faint smile. "Anything for a beautiful woman in need."

For a split second, his gaze lingered on mine, something intense flashing in his expression, but it was gone before I could fully process it. He turned and strode away, leaving me alone to push open the door and step into the room.

Inside, the room was dark except for a small bedside lamp casting a warm glow over the bed. And there, curled up on a soft blanket, was Muffin. Her white-and-gray fur looked a little worse for wear, but she was unmistakably my cat, her ears twitching as she opened one eye and gave me a sleepy look. I let out a breath I didn't realize I'd been holding, rushing over to scoop her up in my arms.

"Muffin," I whispered, nuzzling her as she purred weakly, and relief washed over me like a wave. She was safe, and for the first time in three days, I felt whole.

After a few moments, I heard Hunter's footsteps behind me, and I turned to find him leaning against the doorframe, watching us with that same unreadable expression.

"She likes you," I said, feeling a little silly, but he just shrugged, his eyes never leaving mine.

"Animals tend to. It's humans that are a bit more complicated."

The words hung in the air, and I swallowed, suddenly feeling more aware of the quiet, intimate space around us. Muffin squirmed in my arms, drawing me back to reality.

"I should probably get her home," I murmured, glancing away.

"Of course," he said, but he didn't move. Instead, he took a slow step closer, close enough that I could feel the warmth radiating from him, even in the chill of the storm.

"Maybe I'll check in on her… and you," he added, his voice dropping to a murmur that seemed to echo through the room.

I nodded, unable to tear my eyes away from his. "Thank you, Hunter. I don't know how to repay you."

He reached out, gently brushing a stray lock of hair behind my ear, his fingers lingering just a bit too long. "Let's just say you owe me," he said, a smile playing on his lips.

As I gathered Muffin and moved to the door, I couldn't shake the feeling that my relief was quickly being replaced by something else entirely—a strange, electric thrill that had nothing to do with the storm raging outside.

Chapter 10

When I got back to my car, I could barely believe it—no matter how many times I tried, it wouldn't budge. The wheels spun uselessly in the mud, sinking deeper with every attempt. After several frustrated pushes on the gas, I realized I was stuck. Muffin blinked up at me from the passenger seat as if to say, This is what you get for making me come out in this storm.

I sighed, resigned, and gathered her in my arms. My only choice was to head back inside. Hunter had said he'd wait up for me, after all. Maybe he'd have some idea of how to get my car out, or at the very least, a place to wait out the storm until it was safe to drive.

The house felt even larger and darker as I approached, its lights casting a warm glow in the rain. I knocked lightly on the door, and Hunter answered almost immediately, his eyes flicking to Muffin and then back to me.

"Car trouble?" he asked, a slight smile tugging at the corner of his mouth.

"Stuck in the mud, unfortunately," I admitted, feeling a little embarrassed. "Is it alright if I stay until the rain stops?"

"Of course." His voice was soft, reassuring. "You're welcome to stay in the guest room. There are fresh clothes in there, and a robe—much better than being soaked all night."

I gave a grateful nod and followed him down the long hallway to a room that looked even cozier than it had before, with an inviting bed and a fluffy robe folded on the end. I set Muffin on the bed, and she settled in immediately, curling into a contented little ball. The sight of her sleeping safely brought a wave of relief over me, and I slipped into the bathroom to change, letting the warmth of the plush robe seep in as I wrung out my hair and hung my wet clothes.

A knock sounded on the door a few minutes later. "Gina?"

"Yes?"

"Would you like some dinner?" he asked, his voice close on the other side of the door. "You must be hungry after being out all day."

My stomach growled at the thought, reminding me that I hadn't eaten since yesterday. I opened the door to find Hunter standing there, looking both polite and amused.

"That sounds wonderful, thank you," I said.

He led me to the dining room, which was set with an intimate spread of food, freshly warmed as if waiting for me all along. As we sat across from each other, he poured us each a glass of deep red wine. I sipped mine, the rich flavor melting away my lingering nerves.

"So, you spend your days rescuing cats, then?" he teased, his green eyes glinting over the rim of his glass.

"Not exactly," I laughed, the warmth of the wine helping me relax. "But Muffin's the closest thing I have to family here. I'd do anything to make sure she's safe."

He nodded, his gaze thoughtful. "That kind of loyalty is rare." He paused, studying me for a beat before refilling my glass.

Between bites, he told me about the house and the land, the years his family had owned it, how it was both a retreat and a place to build a legacy. I listened, enchanted by his low voice and the quiet strength behind his words.

After dinner, he offered me his arm. "Would you like a tour?"

I took it, feeling the warmth of his touch as we wandered through hallways lined with rich wood and gleaming paintings, the house sprawling far beyond what I'd realized from the outside. When his phone rang, he gave a brief sigh.

"Excuse me. I won't be long."

As he answered, I glanced around and noticed a door slightly ajar. It led into a small room lit by the soft glow of recessed lights, with framed paintings covering every wall. I stepped inside, drawn to the vivid brushstrokes and colors that filled the space with life.

Then I saw it. In the center of the room was a painting of a woman, painted with stunning, almost surreal detail. She was sitting by a window, her expression serene, yet there was something in her gaze—a hint of longing, of intensity. I took a step closer, my breath catching as I realized she looked exactly like me.

"Gina." Hunter's voice made me jump, and I turned to see him standing in the doorway, watching me. His expression was unreadable, his eyes dark and intent. He took a slow step into the room, his gaze never leaving mine. "I suppose I should have told you."

His voice was low, steady, almost hypnotic. "I saw you one day in the park, with Muffin, and I couldn't forget you. I painted that from memory before I ever even knew your name."

I felt a shiver run down my spine, a mix of awe and disbelief. "So Muffin going missing..."

He gave a slight, almost regretful smile. "The perfect chance for us to meet. After you posted about her going missing. I searched for her and found her near a coffee shop, hurt and scared so I brought her home,"

His words hung in the air, and my pulse quickened as he stepped closer, his gaze intense and unflinching. Before I could speak, he reached out, tracing a gentle line along my jaw. His touch was electric, sending a warmth through me that settled low and heavy in my stomach.

"Hunter..." My voice was barely a whisper, caught between shock and something else, something undeniable.

His hand slid to the back of my neck, and then his mouth was on mine, his kiss firm, passionate, as though he'd been waiting forever. I melted into him, unable to hold back, my hands sliding up his chest as he pulled me against him, his arms wrapping around me like he'd never let go.

When he pulled back, his gaze burned into mine, his voice husky as he murmured, "Come with me."

Without a second thought, I followed him down the hall, my hand in his, as he led me to his bedroom. The storm raged outside, but here in the warmth of his touch, I felt like I'd been exactly where I was meant to be all along.

Chapter 11

Hunter kissed me as soon as I got into the room, barely closing the door behind us. His lips were urgent, demanding, as he pressed me against the closed door. My fingers tangled in his hair, pulling him closer as the kiss deepened. Hunter's hands roamed down my sides, untying the robe and slipping beneath the thin fabric of my borrowed clothes. His touch left trails of fire on my skin.

He broke the kiss, his breath ragged. "I've dreamed of this," he murmured, his lips trailing down my neck. "Of you."

I gasped as he found a sensitive spot, arching into him. "Hunter," I breathed, barely recognizing my own voice, thick with desire.

In one fluid motion, he lifted me, my legs wrapping around his waist as he carried me to the bed. He laid me down gently, his eyes roaming over me with an intensity that made me shiver. Slowly, reverently, he began to undress me, his fingers tracing each newly exposed inch of skin.

"Beautiful," he whispered, his voice filled with awe. "Even more beautiful than I imagined."

I reached for him, pulling him down to me, desperate to feel his skin against mine. Our bodies moved together in a dance as old as time, yet it felt new, electric, as if we'd discovered something no one else had ever known.

Outside, thunder crashed and lightning illuminated the room in brief flashes, but I was lost in Hunter's touch, in the feel of his body against mine, in the way he whispered my name like a prayer.

The kiss deepened as he slid between my legs, his lips pressing against mine, making my heart race. His tongue traced my bottom lip before slipping inside my mouth, tasting me for the first time. There was something raw, primal about the way he kissed me. As he pulled back, I could feel his breath on my face, his eyes searching mine. He undid his belt slowly and let it fall to the floor with a soft metallic clang.

His fingers traced over the buttons on his shirt, popping them one by one before pulling the fabric apart to reveal his chest. His skin was warm and smooth, and I couldn't help but run my hands along his muscled torso as he lowered himself onto the bed beside me.

His touch was gentle yet firm as he caressed my inner thighs, sending shivers down my spine. He moved closer, pressing his hardness against my core, and I gasped in anticipation. His mouth trailed kisses up my neck and over my shoulder blade, each touch leaving me aching for more.

With a groan, he rolled onto his back pulling me on top of him so that our hips were aligned. He reached between us and stroked himself teasingly against me, and I whimpered at the feeling. He smirked wickedly before lifting one of my legs and placing it over his hip, positioning himself perfectly inside of me.

The slow penetration was both sudden and exquisite, filling me up completely. He gripped my hips tightly as he began to move in slow thrusts that sent shockwaves through both of us.

Our bodies moved together in perfect synchronicity, as if we'd known each other for years rather than hours. Hunter's hands roamed my body, memorizing every curve and plane. His lips trailed fire across my skin, whispering words of adoration between heated kisses. I arched into him, overwhelmed by the intensity of sensation and emotion.

The storm outside seemed to mirror our passion, with flashes of lightning illuminating the room in brief, electric moments. Thunder rumbled, drowning out our gasps and moans. Rain lashed against the windows, but we were lost in our own world, oblivious to anything beyond the feel of skin on skin.

Hunter rolled us over, pinning me beneath him. His eyes locked onto mine, dark with desire but also something deeper - a connection I couldn't fully comprehend but felt to my core. He intertwined our fingers, pressing my hands into the mattress as he drove into me with increasing urgency.

"Gina," he groaned, his voice rough with need. "You're everything I've dreamed of."

I could only respond with breathless cries of pleasure as the tension built within me. Hunter seemed to sense how close I was, adjusting his angle to hit just the right spot. His free hand slipped between us, circling and stroking in time with his thrusts.

The crescendo hit me like a tidal wave. I cried out Hunter's name as waves of ecstasy washed over me. He followed moments later, burying himself inside me.

I gasped as Hunter filled me completely, my body stretching to accommodate him. He held still for a moment, his eyes locked on mine, both of us savoring the sensation of our bodies joined as one. Then he began to move, slow, deep thrusts that made me moan with pleasure.

My hands roamed his broad shoulders, feeling the muscles flex beneath my fingers as he moved above me. Hunter's lips found mine again in a searing kiss, swallowing my cries of ecstasy as he quickened his pace.

The storm outside seemed to match our passion, thunder rumbling as lightning illuminated the room in brief flashes. But I was lost in the storm of sensation Hunter was creating within me, every nerve ending alive and tingling.

"Gina," he groaned, his voice rough with desire. "You feel incredible."

I arched up to meet his thrusts, wrapping my legs around his waist to pull him even deeper. "Hunter," I gasped. "Don't stop."

He shifted slightly, changing the angle, and suddenly stars exploded behind my eyes. I cried out, my nails digging into his back as waves of pleasure washed over me. Hunter's movements became more urgent, more erratic, and I knew he was close.

"Let go," I whispered in his ear. "I've got you."

With a guttural moan, Hunter shuddered above me, his release triggering another climax of my own.

Before I could relish in the pleasure he had given me, Hunter got on his knee's between my legs. He looked up at me smirking before licking my clit, I gasped.

I threw my head back, letting out a long moan that echoed in the room.

His tongue flicked my still sensitive clit.

"That feels so good, Hunter," I moaned.

His breath was hot against my folds as he circled his tongue around the sensitive nub, teasing and tasting me. His fingers moved in time with his tongue, pressing deep inside me and stroking my walls. My hips bucked up towards him, desperate for more of this incredible sensation.

The room was filled with the sounds of our passion: the wet smack of lips, the rough rustle of fabric, the low moans and gasps that escaped our throats.

He shifts slightly, slipping a finger into me and curling it upwards to meet his tongue's movements. I cry out, arching my back off the bed. With each flick of his tongue, I felt new waves of pleasure roll through me, stronger than before. "Hunter," I whimper, unable to form complete thoughts as he drives me closer to the edge.

His lips leave my folds, tracing a path down my inner thighs before he stops at my entrance once again. His fingers slide inside me, finding their way deeper than ever before. He chuckles darkly against my skin and begins thrusting them in and out in rhythm with his tongue's laps at my entrance. It feels like he's consuming me whole - every part of me - and it's glorious.

I dig my nails into his shoulders, holding onto him as if my life depends on it. His muscles flex beneath my touch as he takes me to new heights of pleasure. I throw my head back again, lost in the sensations washing over me.

With one final lick, I came undone.

I collapsed back onto the bed, my chest heaving as waves of pleasure coursed through my body. Hunter crawled up beside me, pulling me close and kissing me deeply. I could taste myself on his lips, and it sent another shiver of desire through me.

"You're incredible," he murmured, his fingers tracing lazy patterns on my skin.

I nestled into his embrace, feeling utterly sated and content. The storm outside had quieted to a gentle patter of rain, matching the calm that had settled over us.

"I can't believe this is real," I whispered, looking up at him. "It feels like a dream."

Hunter smiled, tucking a strand of hair behind my ear. "If it is, I never want to wake up."

Chapter 12

The room was dark, but a soft meow from Muffin pulled me from sleep. She nudged at my hand, insistent and wide awake. I groaned, feeling the lingering warmth of the bed, but sat up anyway, assuming she wanted food.

"All right, Muffin," I whispered, slipping into the robe Hunter had left for me. "Let's get you something to eat."

The house was silent as I made my way through the hall, the storm long since passed, leaving only the gentle hum of rain against the windows. I padded down the stairs, Muffin darting ahead. But she didn't head to the kitchen. Instead, she stopped in front of a small, unassuming door off the main hall, pressing her nose to the crack beneath it and letting out another urgent meow.

I reached for the knob, a sense of unease prickling at the back of my neck. The door opened with a soft creak, and I groped for a light switch, finally flooding the small room with an unforgiving brightness.

My breath caught in my throat.

Photos, files, and papers covered every inch of the wall, all of them with one unmistakable subject: *me*. My face stared back at me from snapshots I didn't even know had been taken—photos of me walking to work, sitting at the park, laughing with friends. And worse, scattered among them were things that shouldn't have been there: a concert ticket I'd thrown away weeks ago, a small trinket I'd lost at a coffee shop, even a dried rose from a bouquet I'd discarded. It was as if every piece of my life had been meticulously collected and stored here.

Muffin meowed again, sensing my unease. I backed up, panic creeping in, clutching her close as I scanned the room, my heart hammering. My mind spun. How could he have all this? And more importantly, why?

I forced myself to move, turning to the door, every nerve on edge. I needed to leave—immediately. But when I returned to the guest room, I froze. My clothes, keys, and phone were gone. Frantically, I searched every corner, throwing open drawers and yanking open the closet, but there was nothing. I was alone, with no way to leave, my connection to the outside world stripped away.

I hurried to the front door, clinging to Muffin. But before I could reach it, I heard a soft, familiar voice behind me.

"Gina." Hunter's voice was smooth, and when I turned, he stood at the top of the stairs, watching me, a knowing smile on his face. "Going somewhere?"

My voice caught in my throat as I tried to speak. "Hunter… I… What is all that? The room… my things…"

He tilted his head, descending the steps slowly, his gaze never leaving mine. "I thought you would've guessed by now," he said, his tone calm, almost affectionate. "From the moment I saw you, Gina, I knew you were meant to be mine."

I backed away, clutching Muffin tighter as he reached the bottom of the stairs. His smile grew, but it wasn't warm. It was the smile of someone who had everything exactly where he wanted it.

"So, you… you let Muffin out?" I whispered, horror dawning over me.

He nodded, unapologetic. "I needed a way to bring you here, somewhere I could finally show you what you mean to me. I didn't think it would be this easy, but you came right to me. It was perfect."

I was frozen, every instinct telling me to run, but my body wouldn't obey. His hands reached out, brushing a strand of hair from my face, and I felt the walls closing in, his touch a cold reminder of just how carefully he'd planned this.

"You don't need to be afraid, Gina," he murmured, leaning in until his face was inches from mine. "This is where you belong. With me."

His lips found mine in a slow, possessive kiss, and though every part of me screamed to fight, I was too shocked, too terrified to move. I felt the weight of his arms wrap around me, a vice-like grip that told me he wasn't planning to let go.

When he pulled back, his eyes gleamed, his voice soft but unyielding. "You're mine, Gina. Forever."

Also by Royal Reeds

Cutting Edge: A BWWM Erotic Romance
Atlas Mercer spent years running—from his past, his enemies, and the ruthless life he left behind as the infamous assassin known only as Obsidian. Now, he's found peace in the last place he ever expected—working in a quiet kitchen, far from the bloodshed. That peace shatters the night he saves Laila Carter, the heir to a powerful business empire, from an ambush that nearly takes her life.

Laila isn't used to relying on anyone, least of all a brooding ex-assassin with dangerous skills and haunted eyes. But with killers closing in and betrayal lurking within her family, Atlas becomes the only person she can trust. Forced into each other's orbit, their tension sparks into undeniable passion—a fire they both know is dangerous but can't resist.

As Atlas uncovers a conspiracy that ties Laila's brother's death to a man she once trusted, he realizes that the enemies hunting them aren't just after her fortune—they want her dead. And the only way to protect her is to become the man he swore he'd never be again.

Tale of Intense Desire

This steamy short story compilation features three sizzling tales that explore the magnetic pull of passion and fantasy. Each story is set in a different place, with characters from diverse backgrounds

The Midnight Encounter

A woman stuck in a loveless marriage decides to explore her fantasies after a chance meeting with a mysterious stranger at a late-night jazz club. What starts as a fleeting conversation awakes a desires she never knew she had.

Desires On The High Seas

A successful businesswoman takes a solo cruise to unwind from her hectic life. She meets a charismatic ship captain who knows how to handle more than just a ship.

The Secret Library

In a city known for its secrets, a secluded library becomes a meeting ground for two book lovers. Their shared passion for rare, erotic literature leads to heated discussions that quickly turn into something more.